Long ago, in the green mountains of China, the village called Beyond the Clouds was ruled by a cruel and clever emperor. But the mountains were high, and the Emperor was far away. The warm climate and fertile soil, and especially the help of a neighbouring elephant family, provided the hard-working farmers with a prosperous and peaceful life. The villagers took great care of the friendly elephants, particularly the baby, Huan-huan.

Huan-huan's mother and father were super-giants; at least, that was what their young keeper, Hei-dou, proudly claimed. Their bulky bodies were taller than any house in the village and thicker than the wall of the Emperor's palace. And their ears were so broad that only the biggest banana leaves could match them.

As for baby Huan-huan, since the day he was born it seemed that every breath of air he took lifted him up an inch and each passing breeze added to his weight.

Every day Hei-dou rose at daybreak and headed out to fetch the elephants. Mother took the lead, closely followed by Hei-dou and Huan-huan, and Father ambled along behind. Their trunks hung casually, their ears flapped to drive away the flies and their flat feet rustled softly on the path to the village.

During the day, while his elephant parents were busy hauling logs, pulling carts, toting bags of grain and barrels of water, or carrying the villagers up on their backs, Huan-huan stayed with Hei-dou and the other schoolchildren. Using his supple trunk, he retrieved balls and shuttlecocks that had landed on the roof and rescued kites and paper birds caught in the trees.

Best of all, when school was out he stood up on his hind feet, fanned his ears and danced, with all the children singing and swirling around him.

At dusk, Huan-huan joined his parents at the shore, where they
drank from the lake, ate succulent green grass and gave each
other a shower or powdered themselves with sand. Hei-dou always
waited and then took them home.

Word of Huan-huan's friendliness and resourcefulness travelled fast and far, and soon reached the palace. Although there were over fifty of the best elephants to carry the Imperial Family and entertain their guests, the Emperor was not satisfied.

"I am the Emperor and I should have the best of everything!" he roared. And he sent his soldiers to bring Huan-huan to him.

"He's only a baby," Hei-dou pleaded with the Emperor's soldiers.

"It's the Emperor's order," growled the captain of the guards, thumping his spear against his shield.

Hei-dou turned to the villagers. "Can't we do something?" he cried. But the farmers stood silently with heads bowed as Huan-huan was taken away.

The angry trumpeting of Huan-huan's mother and father filled the evening sky.

Inside the palace, the young Prince pointed his sword at Huan-huan and screamed, "Show me all your tricks!"

"Water all my flowers," shouted the little Princess, perched on a soldier's shoulders and waving her tiny fists. "Do what I say!"

The Empress's long face was like a twisted rope. "Make the Prince laugh and bring a smile to the Princess," she commanded.

"Obey them or you will be punished," ordered the Emperor, his fat body quaking with every word.

Where are my parents? Huan-
huan wondered. Where are Hei-
dou and the other children? Sad
and confused, he lowered himself to the ground, let out a long
and heavy sigh, and closed his
eyes.

Every day, the Prince shouted himself hoarse, the Princess could hardly keep her eyes dry, the Empress stamped her feet sore with fury and the Emperor's teeth ground so loudly that they could be heard outside the palace wall. But frightened Huan-huan remained frozen to the spot.

One day, Hei-dou led Huan-huan's parents to the palace to beg for their baby's return, only to be chased away by the soldiers long before they approached the gate.

Finally, the angry Emperor decreed an imperial punishment for Huan-huan's disobedience: he was to be heavily chained and sent far, far away, never to see his parents again.

"If the Emperor doesn't want him, why not give him back to the village?" the farmers pleaded with the messenger. "Please ask the Emperor if we can keep him!"

Pulling Huan-huan along behind him with a rope, the messenger returned with a new edict from the palace: "The baby elephant will be taken away in two days unless someone can tell me, the Emperor, how heavy he is."

Hei-dou and the villagers fell silent, for they knew it was a trick. Besides his cruelty and ferociousness, the Emperor was notorious for absurd riddles that often had no solutions.

He had once ordered a fisherman to tell him the number of scales on a live fish. The poor man failed, and the Emperor confiscated his day's catch. The Emperor had also commanded a farmer to count the hairs on his ox. The farmer had no answer, so the ox was slaughtered to feed the Emperor's guests.

A dark cloud shadowed the village. Two days was not much time. Where to start? How to begin?

"Send for the scholars!" someone suggested.

"Bring all the scales to the village square!" another advised.

Quickly the butchers collected their pole-scales, long and short, thin and thick. The shopkeepers brought their counter-scales, round and square, big and small. The farmers pushed the heavy warehouse scales, as tall as Hei-dou's reach and wide as his embrace, into the crowd.

Scholar East broke the silence first, his thin goat-beard moving up and down when he spoke. "Weigh each leg at a time, then add the four numbers."

"Then how can we weigh the elephant?" Hei-dou asked. "How can we save Huan-huan from being sent away?"

"Don't panic," Scholar North said calmly, pointing to the large warehouse scales sitting on the ground. "Place one of his feet on each scale at the same time. *Then* add the four numbers."

"No, no, no, my dear fellow. You forgot his heavy head, long trunk, two fan-like ears and new tusks," sneered Scholar South.

"And his round chubby belly!" Scholar West added.

"What a shame!" Scholar North scolded in a dry voice, shaking his head. "Such silly ideas will never work."

Hei-dou helped the farmers arrange the scales. Once, twice, ten times and twenty, until Hei-dou lost count, poor Huan-huan tried to do as the shouting villagers urged— until suddenly a loud cheer went up as the baby elephant finally managed to balance himself on the scales. But almost immediately a sharp clang rang out as the iron counter-weights sprang into the air and thumped to the ground. Terrified, Huan-huan jumped back off the scales.

Evening came. Sadly Hei-dou said goodbye to
Huan-huan and his parents and walked down to the lake,
hoping that tomorrow would never come. How he wished he could
run off with Huan-huan. But where could they go? Everywhere they
set foot was the Emperor's land. Through tears, he watched the
moon push through the thick clouds and dance above the water,
casting silver light on his father's fishing boat.

Then a thought surged into his mind. He dashed back home and
waited impatiently for dawn to arrive.

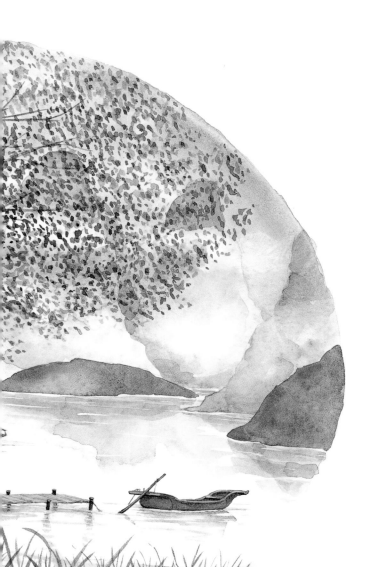

Before sunrise Hei-dou was ready. As he and the plodding elephants walked into the village, people gathered around.

"I know how to weigh Huan-huan," Hei-dou announced.

"How could you succeed where our scholars have failed?" one farmer scoffed.

Another smirked, "You are not even old enough to handle the smallest scale!"

Even his own parents looked doubtful.

"Please," Hei-dou pleaded. "Let me try."

From the distance came the ominous sound of galloping horses.

Hei-dou winked at Huan-huan and whispered into his ear. He then guided the baby elephant to the shore and stopped before his father's boat. At Hei-dou's suggestion, eight strong farmers waded into the lake to hold the boat steady. Gingerly Huan-huan followed Hei-dou along the plank and into the centre of the boat, which quickly settled deep into the water. Hei-dou slipped into the lake and, taking a piece of charcoal from his pocket, carefully drew a solid black line at the water level along the side of the boat.

As soon as he and Huan-huan were back on shore, Hei-dou said loudly, trying to contain his excitement, "Please, everybody, help to carry rice bags into the boat until..."

His father stopped him. "— until the black mark is level with the water again, and..."

"— and," said his mother, "weigh the bags, one at a time, then..."

"— Then add up all the numbers!" another exclaimed.

Everyone chimed in, "The total will be the weight of Huan-huan!"

When the soldiers returned to the palace without Huan-huan and reported what they had seen in the village, the Emperor was speechless.

Red-faced and fuming, he threw the soldiers out and sank into his chair like a deflated balloon. He remained there for the rest of the day, the rest of the week, and the rest of the month. And he never posed another tricky riddle.

Laughter returned to the village, and there were smiles on every face. In the schoolyard, Huan-huan rose up on his hind feet and, encircled by the singing children, began to dance. But that day, it seemed he danced only for Hei-dou.

> Author's note:
>
> The name Hei-dou (pronounced *Hay-dough*) means "black bean".
> Huan-huan's name (pronounced H*wan* as in S*wan*) means "cheerful".

For Bill
—T.Y.

To Samuel, Jean-Remi, David and Alexis
—S.L.

©1998 Ting-xing Ye (text)
©1998 Suzane Langlois (art)
Cover design by Sheryl Shapiro

The Canada Council | Le Conseil des Arts
FOR THE ARTS | DU CANADA
SINCE 1957 | DEPUIS 1957

We acknowledge the support of the Canada Council for the Arts
for our publishing program. We also thank the Ontario Arts Council.

Cataloguing in Publication Data

Ye, Ting-xing, 1952-
Weighing the elephant

ISBN 1-55037-527-X (bound)   ISBN 1-55037-526-1 (pbk.)

I. Langlois, Suzane. II. Title.

PS8597.E16W44 1998   jC813'.54   C98-930309-8
PZ7.Y4We 1998

The art in this book was rendered in watercolours.
The text was typeset in Baskerville.

Distributed in Canada by:
Firefly Books Ltd.
3680 Victoria Park Avenue
Willowdale, ON
M2H 3K1

Published in the U.S.A. by
Annick Press (U.S.) Ltd.
Distributed in the U.S.A. by:
Firefly Books (U.S.) Inc.
P.O. Box 1338, Ellicott Station
Buffalo, NY 14205

Printed and bound in Canada by
Friesens, Altona, Manitoba.

HOW does Science Work?

Magnets and Springs

written by

Carol Ballard

WAYLAND

Published in paperback in 2014 by Wayland
Copyright © 2014 Wayland

Hachette Children's Books
338 Euston Road, London NW1 3BH

Editors: Laura Milne and Camilla Lloyd
Senior Design Manager: Rosamund Saunders
Design and artwork: Peta Phipps
Commissioned Photography: Philip Wilkins
Consultant: Dr Peter Burrows
Series Consultant: Sally Hewitt

Ballard, Carol
    Magnets and springs. - (How does science work?)
    1.Magnets - Juvenile literature 2.Springs (Mechanism) -
    Juvenile literature
    I.Title
    538.4

ISBN-13: 978-0-7502-8246-8

Printed and bound in China

10 9 8 7 6 5 4 3 2 1

Acknowledgements:

Cover photograph: Spring, Colin Cuthbert/Science Photo Library

Photo credits: Richard Megna/Fundamental/Science Photo Library 4, Michael S. Yamishita/Corbis 6, Charles Gullung/Getty Images 10, Cordelia Molloy/Science Photo Library 14, Tom Van Sant/Geosphere/Corbis 16, Roy Mehta/Getty Images 20,Foodfolio/Alamy 21, PE Reed/Getty Images 22, Colin Cuthbert/Science Photo Library 24, Brad Mitchell/Alamy 26.

The author and publisher would like to thank the models Alex Babatola, Sabiha Tasnim, Zarina Collins, Sophie Campbell and Philippa Campbell, and Moorfield School, Ilkley, for the loan of equipment.

Contents

Words in **bold** can be found in the glossary on p.30

Magnets

Magnets have special **properties**. They can **attract** each other, so that they **pull** towards each other. They can also **repel** each other, so that they **push** away from each other. Magnets can also attract some other materials to them.

Magnets have two ends, each end is called a **pole**. One end is the north pole and the other is the south pole.

Most magnets are made from iron, which is a metal. Magnets come in different shapes and sizes.

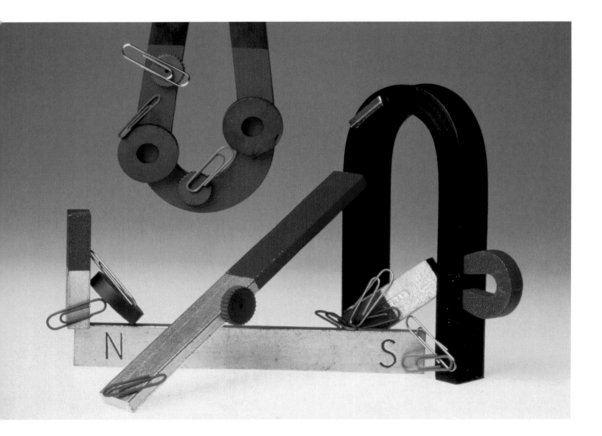

TRY THIS! Investigate magnets

1 You need two bar magnets, the ones used here have one blue end and one red end each.

2 Hold one in each hand.

3 Slowly bring the red ends closer to each other. What can you feel?

4 Now slowly bring the two blue ends closer to each other.

5 Does it feel the same or different?

6 Now bring one red end and one blue end together. How does that feel?

You should find that the blue and red ends are attracted to each other. Two blue ends or two red ends will repel each other.

Comparing magnets

Some magnets are stronger than others and it is not always the biggest magnet that is the strongest.

Different magnets are good for different jobs. Strong magnets are needed to attract heavy objects such as old cars and pieces of machinery. Weaker magnets can be used to attract lighter objects such as pins and paperclips.

This strong magnet attracts metal from other materials in order to collect the metal and recycle it. →

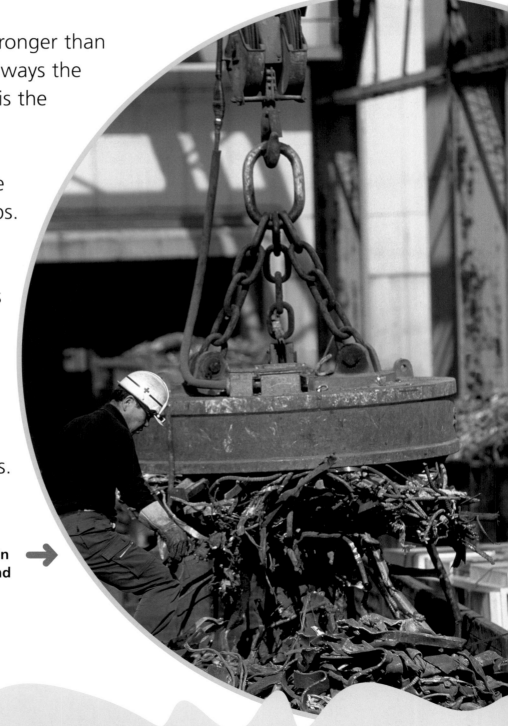

TRY THIS! Test the strength of magnets

1 Find five different magnets.

2 You could choose magnets of different shapes, such as a ball, horseshoe, bar, disc and strip.

3 Put your first magnet by the 0cm mark on a ruler.

4 Put a metal paperclip at the 20cm mark.

5 Slide the paperclip one centimetre towards the magnet. Let go of the paperclip.

6 Does the paperclip move towards the magnet?

You should find that some magnets attract the paperclip from further away than others. These are the strongest magnets.

Is it magnetic?

Something that is attracted to a magnet is called a **magnetic material**. Not all metals are magnetic. Only the metals iron, nickel and cobalt are magnetic. Iron is a common metal and is used to make many things, such as paperclips, fridge doors and some parts of cars. Iron is often mixed with other metals. Cobalt and nickel are much less common.

All other materials are **non-magnetic**. Magnets do not repel non-magnetic materials – they just have no effect on them at all.

These metal chips contain iron and so they are magnetic.

TRY THIS! Find magnetic materials

1 Choose ten objects around you that are made from different materials.

2 Slowly bring a magnet towards the object to see whether it is attracted to it.

3 Test the other objects in turn.

4 Sort the materials into two groups – a magnetic group and a non-magnetic group.

You should find that only objects made from metals are magnetic. These must contain some iron, cobalt or nickel. You might also find that some of your metals are non-magnetic. These will not contain any of those three metals.

Using magnets

Magnets have many different uses. In the home, some door catches use magnets. You can stick small magnets onto metal surfaces like fridges for decoration, to hold lists or to help you to learn. Strong magnets are found in factories and recycling centres. They can be used to sort magnetic materials from non-magnetic materials and to pick up heavy things made from magnetic materials.

Wow!

Electric motors, microphones, loudspeakers, telephones and video recorders all use magnets to work!

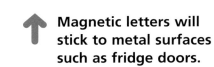
Magnetic letters will stick to metal surfaces such as fridge doors.

TRY THIS! A fishing game

1   You will need a magnet, a stick and some string for each player, a pile of metal paperclips and some card.

2   Draw lots of fish outlines on your card and cut them out.

3   Attach a paperclip onto one side of each fish.

4   Tie a magnet onto one end of the string.

5   Tie the other end onto a stick. Make a fishing rod for each player.

6   With your fishing rod try fishing for your magnetic fish.

You should find that your magnet attracts the paperclips attached to your fish. The magnets pick up the magnetic fish.

Take care using scissors

Magnetism

Inside a magnet there are millions of tiny pieces. Each piece behaves like a mini-magnet. They are all lined up so that all the north poles point one way and the south poles point the opposite way.

Magnetic materials contain mini-magnets too but they are mixed up. When you put a magnet close to the magnetic material, the mini-magnets line up. We say the material is **magnetised**.

In a **temporary magnet**, the mini-magnets slowly get mixed-up again and the magnet loses its **magnetism**. In a **permanent magnet** they stay lined up and magnetic.

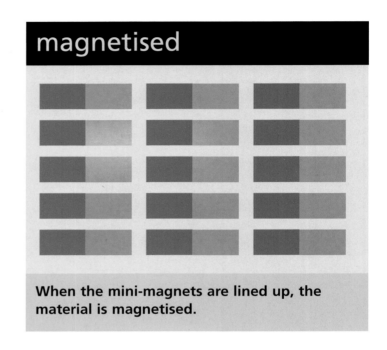

magnetised

When the mini-magnets are lined up, the material is magnetised.

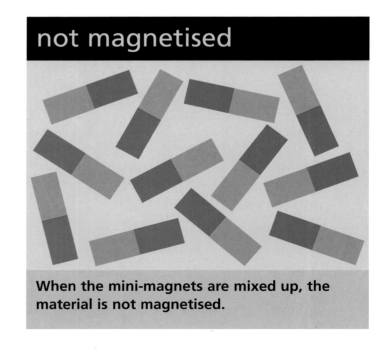

not magnetised

When the mini-magnets are mixed up, the material is not magnetised.

TRY THIS! Make a magnet

1   You will need a metal paperclip and a magnet.

2   Gently stroke it from top to bottom with a magnet 50 times in the same direction.

3   Keep your magnet well away from the paperclip between strokes.

4   Your paperclip should now attract other magnetic materials.

You should find that you have made the paperclip into a magnet. You have lined up the mini-magnets inside it to make a temporary magnet.

Magnetic fields

Magnets can attract magnetic materials without touching them. They produce a force called magnetism, which works in the space around the magnet.

The **magnetic field** is the space around the magnet. The magnet will attract any magnetic materials inside the magnetic field. Magnetism is strongest around the poles of the magnet and weakest around the centre of the magnet.

The iron filings show the pull of the magnetic field around a magnet. →

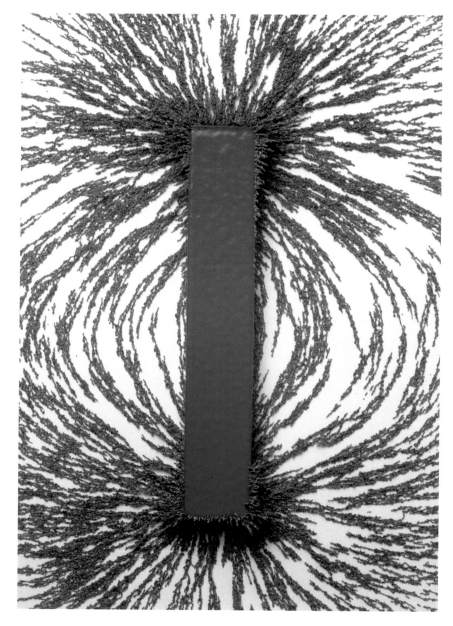

TRY THIS! Investigate magnetic fields

1 You will need some card, a magnet and some iron filings.

2 Put a piece of stiff card on top of a magnet.

3 Carefully, sprinkle some iron filings on top of the card.

4 Look at the pattern the iron filings make.

The iron filings move because the force of magnetism works through the card. The pattern of the iron filings shows you where the magnetic fields are around the magnet.

You can use Blu-Tack or plasticine to remove the iron filings from the magnets but make sure you throw it away after use.

! **Wash your hands after touching iron filings**

Natural magnets

The Earth behaves in the same way as a giant bar magnet. It has its own magnetic field that spreads out into space. The magnetic field is strongest at the poles and weakest around the centre.

Hundreds of years ago, people discovered that they could use the Earth's magnetic field to help them find their way. If a magnet is allowed to hang or float freely, the magnet's South pole will point towards the Earth's North pole. They used this idea to make a simple **compass**, which sailors used to help them find their way. People still use compasses today.

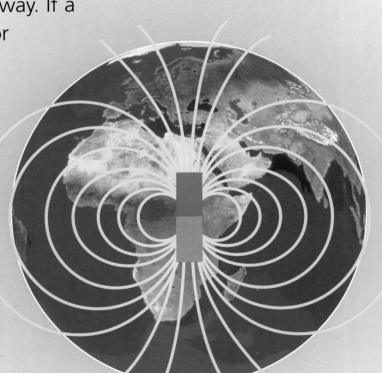

The Earth behaves like a giant magnet with its own magnetic field.

TRY THIS! Make a compass

1 Gently stroke a paperclip with a magnet 50 times, keeping your magnet well away from the paperclip between strokes.

2 Lay the paperclip carefully onto a bowl of water so that it floats.

3 Your paperclip will spin round and eventually settle to point in one direction.

4 Hold a compass up to the saucer.

One end of the paperclip will point north and the other will point south. This is because you have made it into a temporary magnet, which will settle with its poles pointing to the Earth's poles.

Springs

Springs are coils that can be squashed or stretched. When you let go, they spring back into their normal shape. Most springs are made from metal. Springs can be long or short, fat or thin. They can be made from thick wire or thin wire.

If the two ends of a spring are pulled, the spring will **stretch**. Some springs are strong and need a big pulling **force** to stretch them. Others are weaker and can be stretched with a smaller pulling force. When a spring is stretched, we say it is under **tension**.

The coils of the springs can be tightly or loosely packed together.

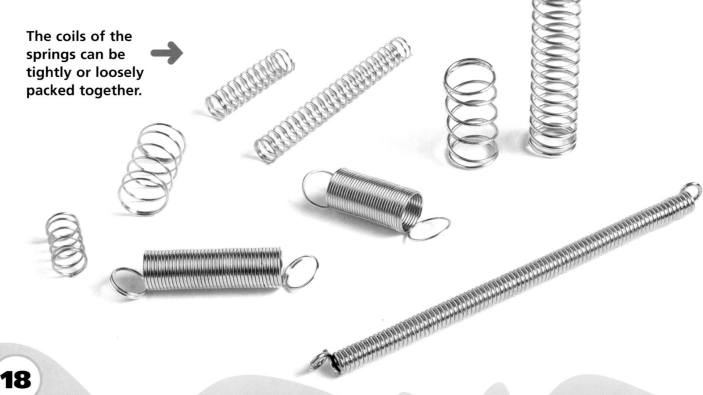

If the two ends of a spring are pushed, the spring will be squashed. Strong springs need a big pushing force to **squash** them. Weaker springs can be squashed with a smaller pushing force. When a spring is squashed, we say it is **compressed**. As soon as you stop pushing on the spring, the spring goes back to its normal shape.

Sometimes, a weak spring can be pulled so hard that it stops behaving like a spring. It just stays stretched and cannot go back to its normal shape.

Some springs can be squashed between your fingers. →

19

Using springs

Springs are used for many different things. We stretch some springs to use them.

A trampoline has springs around its edges. When you land in the middle, the springs are stretched. As they go back to their normal shape, you are pushed up into the air.

 Springs around this trampoline stretch when you land on it.

We squash some springs to use them. For example, some mattresses have springs inside them. When you lie on them, you squash them. When you get up, they go back to their normal shape. The springs make the mattress feel soft and comfortable.

These scales work because when something is put on them, a spring inside is squashed and makes the pointer move. →

Wow!

Train carriages, staplers and push-top biros all have springs in them!

Push and pull

Whatever you do to a spring, it does the same back. To stretch a spring, there must be a pulling force on both ends. These pulling forces must be in opposite directions. When the spring is stretched, it pulls back towards its centre. Whatever the size of your pull, the spring pulls back with exactly the same size pull.

To squash a spring, there must be a pushing force on both ends. These pushing forces must be in opposite directions. When the spring is squashed, it pushes back towards its ends. Whatever the size of your push, the spring pushes back with exactly the same size push.

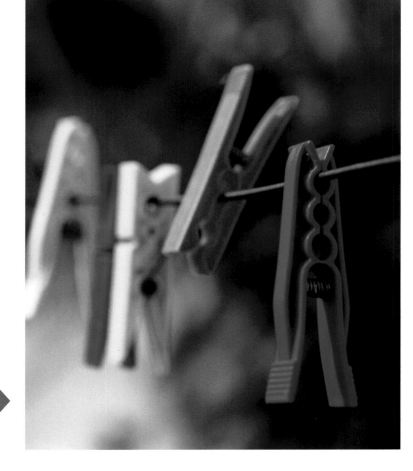

When you push the ends of the clothes peg together the spring is squashed. As you let go the same size force pushes back to close the peg. →

TRY THIS! Push and pull a spring

1 Find a spring you can stretch.

2 Gently stretch the spring a little.

3 Can you feel it pulling back?

4 The more you stretch the spring the more you should feel it pull back.

Now find a spring you can squash. Gently squash the spring. Can you feel it pushing back? If you squash it more you should feel it pushing back more strongly.

Stretching springs

Springs uncoil when they are stretched. A spring is made from metal wire wound into coils. When a spring is stretched, there is no change in the length of metal or the number of coils. What changes is the distance between the coils.

When a spring is stretched, the coils are pulled further apart.

A **forcemeter** contains a spring that can be stretched. When you hold the top of the forcemeter and hang an object on the hook, the object pulls the hook down. This stretches the spring inside. You can read the size of the pulling force by reading the scale on the side of the forcemeter.

TRY THIS! Stretch a forcemeter's spring

1 Measure the length of the spring inside a forcemeter.

2 Hang a mug or a pencil case on the end and measure the length of the spring again.

3 Subtract your first measurement from this measurement to find how many centimetres the spring has stretched.

4 Now add a different object and measure the spring again.

Subtract your first measurement again to find out how many centimetres the spring has stretched this time. You should find that the heavier the object the more the spring will stretch.

You can use a forcemeter to investigate stretching springs.

Squashing springs

When you squash a spring, you push its coils closer together. The spring will seem shorter but there is no change in the length of metal or the number of coils.

When the spring is stretched, the coils are pulled further apart. The spring will look longer but there will still be the same number of coils. There is just more space between each coil.

There is a spring inside this Jack in a Box. It is squashed when the lid is shut but pushes the toy up when the lid opens.

TRY THIS! Make a pop-up card

1   You will need some card, a spring, scissors and some Blu-Tack.

2   Fold a piece of card in half.

2   On one side decorate the front of your card.

Take care using scissors

3   Make a flower or animal shape from another piece of card.

4   Attach the spring to the animal or flower and stick it in the inside of the card with Blu-Tack or cellotape.

6   Shut the card.

When you open it the spring should pop up with your shape on the end!

Stretchy materials

Stretchy materials have similar properties to springs. Some materials will stretch and then go back to their original shape. These materials are **elastic materials**. For example, rubber bands will go back to their original shape after they have been stretched. Other materials, like plasticine can stay in their new shape. Materials like this are not elastic.

These things are all made from elastic materials.

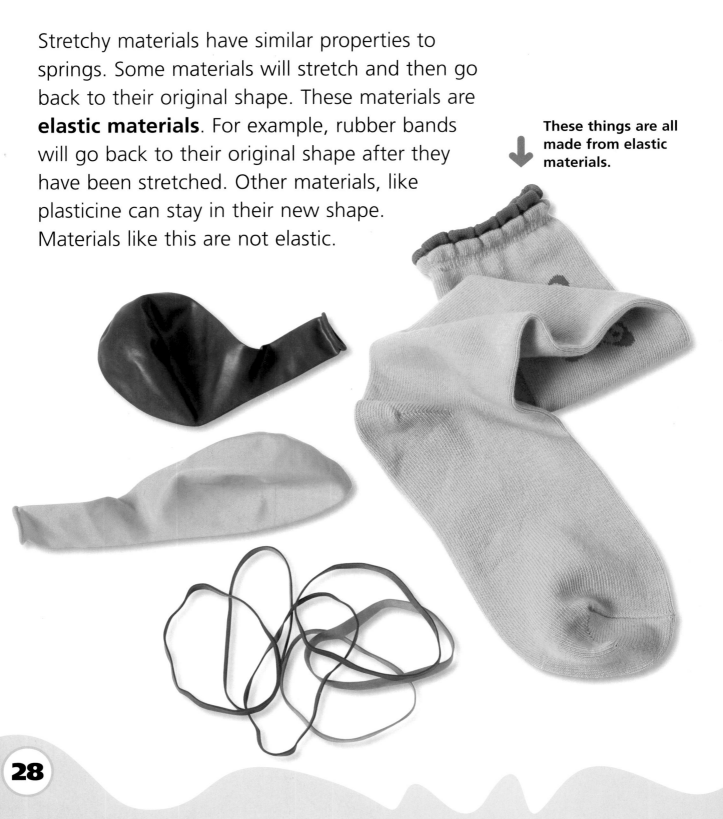

TRY THIS! Investigate stretchy materials

1　Collect together some materials that can be stretched, such as a piece of elastic, a rubber band, an unused balloon or some old tights.

2　Stretch each material against a ruler.

3　You can make a chart of how far each material stretched.

Which material stretched the most? Which material stretched the least? Did any materials stay stretched or were they all elastic materials?

You should find that the elastic materials spring back to their original shape.

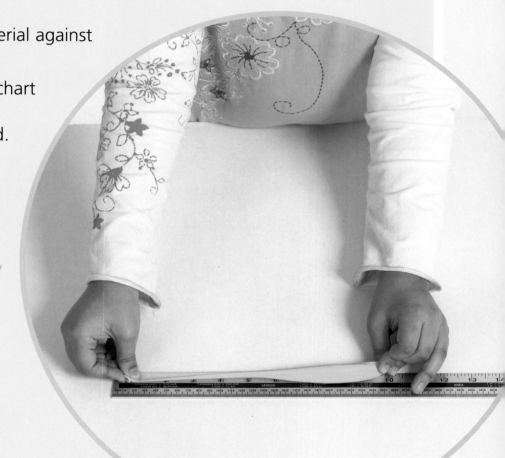

Glossary

attract pull towards

compass an instrument that tells you which direction you are facing

compressed when a spring is squashed

elastic materials materials that go back to their original shape after being stretched

force a push or a pull

forcemeter an instrument for measuring forces

magnetic material a material that acts like a magnet

magnetic field the space around a magnet where its magnetic force works

magnetised materials that become magnetic

magnetism the force that pulls magnetic materials towards a magnet

magnets objects that attract magnetic materials to them

non-magnetic a material that does not act like a magnet, and is not affected by a magnet

permanent magnet a magnet that is always magnetic

pole one end of a magnet

properties what a material is like

pull force used to stretch a spring or stretchy material

push force used to squash a spring or stretchy material

repel push away

springs coils of wire that can be stretched or squashed

squash get shorter

stretch get longer

temporary magnet a magnet that quickly loses its magnetism

tension the pull in a spring or stretchy material when it is stretched